TWILIGHT CRUISE

Mary's Story

Ian Wilson

Cover design by: I Wilson

CONTENTS

CHAPTER ONE:

Born in 1930 in the Wavertree area of Liverpool, Mary Jones is a sweet old lady with a gritty streak, thinning grey hair, a weary deep lined face and a distinct browning around her lips from the nicotine of twenty cigarettes a day for god knows how many years. She can be a lady when she needs to be, but she has a gob that could strike fear into the best of men and the wherewithal to pack a mean kick with her size six, Velcro strapped, slippers.

Mary married her childhood sweetheart, Eddie, in 1952, at the tender age of twenty-two. Eddie, or Ed as she called him, is a quiet reserved man, tall and slim, always well dressed in pristine white ironed shirt and pressed trousers, his once thick black hair has now receded and is no more than a band of grey spikes across the back of his head. Although ninety-one years old he still feels he has to hide the fact he's lost his locks and is very rarely seen without his flat cap on.

Sitting in the living room of their little bungalow in a quiet close in Huyton, on the outskirts of Liverpool, Mary is chatting to her sister on the phone, she's been on for at least 40 minutes repeating the same conversation they had yesterday, and the day before. After several attempts she finally manages to finish her call, and shouts through to the kitchen "EDDIE, put the kettle on our Margi's on her way round, she's got a surprise for us."

"Bloody hell woman, you've been speaking to her for an hour, couldn't she tell ya over the phone"

Eddie starts shuffling around the kitchen muttering to himself. "What are you muttering about you old sod?"

"The surprise'll be that she sods off before the final of strickly dancin comes on, she'll be here all bloody night as usual, an there'll only be one idiot makin the tea."

Margi is Mary's younger sister, eighteen years younger almost to the day, She was divorced from her long-suffering husband Eric years ago after he found her in bed with the postman's dog, although Eric wouldn't have known it was the postman's dog if he hadn't found the postman half naked in the wardrobe. She still insists it was a mistake and the dog had bit the poor posty and ripped his pants off; she swears she was just trying to help get them back on when Eric had walked in.

"Here's our Margi, is that kettle boiled?" Eddie comes through with the tea and plonks it down on the coffee table before heading back towards the kitchen to get out of the way.

"Two sugars, stirred to the right and tap the spoon on the side love" Margi barked at him.

"Kiss my backside and do it yourself, the sugars on the tray."

Margi and Mary sit for a while reminiscing about when the two were younger and used to enjoy the odd night out at the Grafton, which is a well-known night club in Liverpool where every night was grab-a-granny night.

"Eh Marg, remember that fella from Huyton with the dodgy eye? We used to say he had one eye in Huyton and the other in Brighton an every time he heard us he'd go off his head. Them were the days eh!"

"Yeah, if I had a quid for every time he looked straight at me, I'd be 50p better off today!

The pair of them creased up laughing, tears running down their cheeks, and Eddie managed a little giggle to himself in the kitchen, he'd never heard that one before.

The two talked for hours on end about their youth and how they'd love to relive some of those great times.

"Remember that time me and Ed met up with ya for that blind date? I think his name was Alan, we walked into the Red Lion and he was sitting there with a big bunch of flowers and a white carnation in the lapel of his crimson red, velvet jacket, looking like one of Santa's little helpers and you refused to go over. Wonder if he's still sitting there?"

"Dya know what Mary, I'm sure I saw him in town the other week, he was with a woman who used to go the bingo. Looks like he's got a few quid now as well, can't have everything though can ya!"

Mary would bring Eddie into the conversation at every chance because he had been her life from the age of seventeen and she would continually go back to when the two of them would go dancing and the times they had caravanning in Wales for their summer holidays, mainly at their favourite little camp site in Pwllheli with a view over the sea and a great little pub where they used to meet friends they'd met over the years, or their weekend trips to Pontins in Southport with Margi and Eric, Eric being the ex-husband that doesn't like postmen anymore.

Mary shouted through to the kitchen, "Do you remember those weekends Ed, they were great times?"

"Yes, I remember they used to get all the army lads there. Margi had a thing for men in uniform then, didn't realise it stretched to postmen though"

"Cheeky bugger, he didn't have a uniform on last time I seen him"

Eddie and Mary would constantly talk about the years that have passed and both agreed that they wouldn't change anything in their lives and would love to do it all again if they had the chance.

After a while Margi finally came around to the reason that she had called, she shouted Eddie to come through for the announcement.

It was Mary's 90th birthday soon and her and Eddie's wedding anniversary in the next few weeks and Margi had seen an advert in the Liverpool Echo for something that she thought would be a lovely present.

"Can I have a drum roll?" Margi pounded on the coffee table and

7

then proudly announced "I've booked you a cruise for the elderly."

Eddie looked at her like she'd lost her mind, "A bloody cruise, on a ship, in the sea, we're too bloody old for that sort of thing."

Margi went on to explain it was an organised cruise for older people and everyone on the ship would be around their age.

"It's called Twilight Cruises" she added.

Eddie piped up again "It's a bunch of geriatrics on a floating coffin is what it is! Twilight cruises my backside!"

Ignoring Eddie's outburst, Margi explained that she'd booked them a cabin high up on the ship because she thought they might be a bit scared if they were too close to the water and were too low down, Eddie let out a groan and said "so if the boat turns over we'll be at the bottom. Are you trying to get rid of us?."

Eddie was told to stop moaning and Margi went on to say, "I've already paid for it, so you'll have to go or I'll lose my money."

Although still not convinced the couple finally agreed to give it a go, it's obviously not going to be as good as Pwllheli, but it might be OK.

The next few weeks were spent getting their holiday bags packed in anticipation of the old folks' cruise as Eddie persisted in calling it. Mary packed her best dresses for the formal evenings and made sure they had the right money for the trip while Eddie spent his time running around for everything and anything that Mary thought they might need.

He'd never been in and out of Tesco's and Asda so many times in his life, he told Mary that if he kept going there that he'd be inviting the staff home for dinner, I'm getting to know them all by name now. You'd have thought they were going for three months instead of eight days.

As it got closer the couple were really starting to look forward to it. They could feel the excitement building, but also the apprehension.

Finally, the day arrived, and they get up extra early to make sure that everything is packed.

Eddie starts to check through the cases and finds six packets of biscuits, four pot noodles and a sleeve of penguins, "What are all these for, won't they have food on the ship?"

"You never know when one of us might take ill and be stuck in the room love, better to be safe than sorry"

"Can't the other one go to get food, or get room service to bring it?"

"Just leave them in there, I feel better knowing we won't starve"

The wait is finally over, Margi pulls up outside to pick them up to take them to the docks at Liverpool for the start of their journey.

On the way there they pass some of the places and iconic buildings that they'd frequented when they were younger. The Eagle and Child pub in Page Moss, now an Aldi and McDonalds, the old Mecca bingo hall in Dovecot, Dovecot baths, flattened and now houses. The Greyhound pub, now a KFC and the Knotty Ash pub, which is now a pine furniture shop. All those years of memories gone, such a shame.

All the way down Prescot Road into town buildings had disappeared, including Alder Hey Hospital, it's now a fancy, state of the art place with grass on the roof, used to be a beautiful old building.

They enter town and pass the buildings and places they used to go when they were kids. They commented on how the old buildings brought back great memories from when they were young, St. Georges Hall and the museum "Eddie; remember we used to go there for a day out, then down into St. Johns market for a few hours"

"Yep, St' Johns ain't the same anymore as it was back then, I miss them days.

Mary stares out of the window and says "Dya know what Ed, so do I, nothing's the same anymore, everything is rush, rush, rush, and all this new technology ruined the community spirit. Nobody talks anymore."

Margi butts in with "It's them bloody mobile phones, everyone walks round with one stuck in their face, funny they haven't all got humpty backs and square friggin eyes."

CHAPTER TWO:

Arriving at the dock they were amazed by the size of the ship, it was a glorious sight, pure white hull with layers and layers of glass balconies and porthole windows that looked like a pearl necklace around the ship. With the sun glistening off the balconies it was like a gigantic wedding cake, sitting on a platter of the murky waters of the Mersey.

It was so much bigger than they had imagined; They'd never been on anything bigger than the Mersey Ferry, Mary remarked that It seemed to go on forever, "We'll never get time to go around the whole thing if we stay on for a month."

There were hundreds of people boarding, many of them in wheelchairs and using walking aids, some using mobility scooters and some, although not many, walking up the gang plank.

Eddie didn't seem overly impressed that he would be spending the next eight days with people who made him look young, "It's like a scene from Cocoon" he said before they said their farewells to Margi and set off to navigate customs and then heading up the gang plank themselves to embark on their first ever cruise at the age of almost ninety and ninety-one. It was all getting very exciting for Mary she couldn't wait to meet her fellow passengers for their trip into the unknown.

Once on-board Eddie and Mary made their way to their cabin, "112, 114, 116, here it is love 116, have ya got the key?." It was more than acceptable, extremely well fitted out with a queen bed and all the hanging space that they could possibly need, an en suite bathroom and Mary couldn't help but notice the quality of the sheets, lovely white Egyptian cotton. "Eddie, I think I might enjoy staying in this room, it's a real home from home"

After freshening up the pair stepped out into the corridor. "Which way do we go Ed? I'm lost already."

"The room was on ar left, so turn right and we'll get back to the lifts, I think!"

They worked it out and headed up to the top deck for the sail away from Liverpool, they found themselves a nice comfortable seating area and ordered a couple of drinks. Eddie had his usual pint of bitter and Mary thought she'd spoil herself with a gin and tonic, they are on holiday after all.

The ships horn gave an almighty blast signalling that the ship would soon be on its way. Mary and Eddie made their way to the port side to wave to Margi who had waited at the port until they were leaving. There were hundreds of people on the dock waving their respective relatives away, so it took them a while to find Margi in the crowd. Mary shouted "There she is in the red jacket, the one I bought her for Christmas last year" Eddie smiled and thought to himself that was the one she borrowed last year and never gave back.

There was a little bit of a judder as the huge engines were put under pressure to get them moving and they were on their way, the top deck was filled with people mulling about and there was a sing along with the entertainment team, singing all the old songs, which everyone was joining in with. Vera Lynn, Dean Martin, Old Blue Eyes, each song bringing with it its own memories. Everyone chatting about where they were from, stories about their children and their grandchildren and some with great grandchildren. Unfortunately, Eddie and Mary had never had children, Mary had been taken ill as a child with Rubella and found out at an early age that she would never bear children. This had always been something that they didn't really speak about but was always there in the back of their minds.

A few drinks later and the Captain arrived on deck bearing a shiny brass badge adorned with Captain Kenneth P Thomson, he was chatting with people and sharing his knowledge of the ship. Captain Thomson was a short and slightly chubby man with a happy looking face, he wore his snow-white uniform with such pride, every crease was perfect, and every button shone like a precious jewel. He was impeccably dressed, and from his demeanour, he obviously knew it.

He eventually reached the area where Mary was seated and asked if he could sit with her for a while, which she was of course overwhelmed by. "I've never spoke to a Captain before, should I curtsey?" He laughed and began to ask Mary about her trip and how she had ended up on that particular cruise.

After explaining how her sister had booked it for Eddie and herself she went on to tell him how Margi had called to tell them about the cruise and ended up reminiscing about their youth, which led onto her telling him the story of how she and Eddie had met.

He wanted to hear more so Mary expanded on the story telling him how she was fifteen and Eddie was sixteen when they first spoke at school in Liverpool and how he finally plucked up the courage to ask her on a date two years later. "He asked me to a dance in the local hall and he picked me up on his brother's motorbike, I thought he was a real dish in his tight jeans and denim jacket from Flemmings. He had locks of black hair and the widest smile I had ever seen. We were married in 1952 at the Church of All Saints in Liverpool, it was a beautiful wedding with all our friends and family there, and we had our honeymoon in a caravan in Pwllheli in North Wales." She told him how Eddie worked on the docks in Liverpool most of his life and worked his way up to a management position, and she had worked in the Meccano factory in Wavertree until she retired in 1992. I fell in love with him from the first moment we met, and we have never been apart from that day to this.

The Captain seemed really moved by her story and asked if she would do it all again given the chance, without hesitation she replied "Yes, without a doubt, and twice over."

Eddie arrived back from the bar with the drinks and Mary introduced him to the Captain. He immediately began to ask the Captain whether they had done this twilight cruise before and if so how many survivors did they bring back, after all most of the passengers were either on wheels or sticks, one big wave and it could be carnage, with sticks and wheels everywhere, it would be like a pile up on the road into Skegness.

The Captain smiled and informed him that they had in fact done many twilight cruises for the elderly and they had never lost a passenger yet, if anything the passengers came back healthier and more youthful than when they left, he then leaned over to Mary kissed her on the cheek and whispered "Enjoy your journey, I hope it's as good as you wished for."

After the Captain had moved on, Mary turned to an elderly lady who was sitting to her side. "Looking forward to it? she asked. The lady leaned forward and asked Mary to repeat what she'd said, "I'm a bit deaf love, my hearing aid is on the other side, you'll need to speak up." Mary leaned toward her and asked again slightly louder this time "Are you looking forward to it?"

"No need to shout love, I'm only here" was the response.

"Well you said you were deaf, so I spoke louder"

"Just my little joke, makes people a bit more relaxed when they think they've got one over on ya. My name's June, what's yours?"

"Mary, and this is Eddie, what's your fella's name?"

"Joe, but he's a miserable auld git, you'll be lucky to get two words out of him"

June and Mary struck up a conversation and chatted for a good half an hour before Mary turned back to Eddie and said, "So what dya think then, shall we go with em or not?"

Eddie had no idea what she was on about but knew the answer was yes, if it was no Mary would be glaring at him as she asked.

Eddie and Mary had another drink and headed off to their cabin, on the way Eddie asked Mary where they were going with the woman she was talking to. "Weren't you listening"

"Errr. No!, you were rabbiting for that long I had a nap"

"We're going for a drink with them tomorrow night"

They reached their cabin and got into bed, Eddie switched off the light and before long Mary was listening to the rhythmic sounds of Eddie snoring while she lay awake wondering what the Captain meant when he'd said I hope it's as good a journey as you wished for. She hadn't mentioned that she wished to go on a cruise?

Sitting in bed listening to Eddie's nasal opera she started to cast her mind back to some of the things they'd done together over the years, the good times and the bad, although the good far out-weighed the bad.

Eddie had been a wonderful husband and a great man; she had been spoiled with his love over the years and even when they had nothing he gave her everything he had. His love was so special, and it had helped get them through any rough patches they had endured.

Slowly Mary began to nod off with the thoughts of their long and happy lives together lingering in her mind. She laid down and gently dropped into a deep sleep.

CHAPTER THREE:

In the morning Mary awoke to a darkened room and reached over to turn on the bedside lamp, the light came on and Mary immediately thought something wasn't quite right, the room seemed different, much darker walls and the lighting seemed a lot dimmer than the night before. She turned to wake Eddie but what she saw made her let out an almost silent scream. There was a young dark-haired man in the bed beside her and she was afraid that she might wake him.

She crept out of the bed and with her back to the wall edged her way towards the door whispering to herself "What have I done? A couple of gin and tonics and I've turned into Mrs Robinson, oh my God, what will Eddie say?"

She finally arrived at the door and opened it as quietly as she could checking the number on the outside of the cabin door. "116, that's our cabin, who is that in our bed? and where's my Eddie? What the hell have I done?"

As she closed the door and made her way towards the closet, she heard the man speak. "Mary, what are you doing, come back to bed." She recognised the voice but couldn't quite place it, then it dawned on her. That was Eddie's voice, but not Eddie's voice, it sounded like Eddie but from many years ago before he got the croak in his voice.

"Oh my giddy aunt, is that you Eddie?" "Course it's me love, who was you expecting? Come back to bed" was the response.

Mary made her way slowly to the bathroom, but it was no longer an en suite, it was just a sink and towel rail with a mirror over the sink. She glanced at the mirror and caught her reflection, which made her spin around with fear that another woman was standing behind her. Her heart racing, she spun around again, nobody there, she glanced again at the mirror and looking straight back at her was a twenty year old Mary.

"It's a dream, just a bloody dream. I just need to wake up and all will be back to normal" Mary began to pinch herself as hard as she could trying to wake herself but to no avail so she switched on the tap and began to swill her face with cold water, "That'll wake me up." Eddie asked her what all the commotion was about and she replied, "It's ok I'm just waking myself up love, it'll all be fine in a minute."

She stopped, took a step back from the sink and gave out an almighty scream, which made Eddie bolt out of the bed and the cabin attendant come knocking on the door. Eddie opened the door and explained to the cabin attendant that his wife had been having a bad dream. He then turned to Mary and asked what on earth she was doing.

"You look very young" she said "like you did when I met you" Eddie answered her with "I only met you 5 years ago love. Are you having a funny turn, maybe the ships food doesn't agree with you, do you need the doctor?"

He suggested that they get dressed and go for breakfast, maybe then she'd remember where we are.

Mary went to the closet and looked for her summer dress, she'd packed it for ease of dressing before breakfast or going to the pool, what she found was a wardrobe full of clothes which she quickly realised were the clothes she wore in the early 50's following the war. If this is a dream it's certainly realistic, it had to be a dream, but then she was enjoying it so much, having her clothes she used to love and seeing Eddie as he was when they met. She thought, I can't wait to wake up I'll call our Margi and tell her all about this, but in the meantime I'm going to enjoy myself.

On the way to the breakfast hall they passed a number of people all in their early to mid twenties and Mary recognised some of them from the night before except the night before they were in wheelchairs and on Zimmer frames and sticks. Everyone was acting like there was nothing untoward, but Mary knew it was just a dream, it had to be, she can't have travelled back in time, that's not possible, is it?

Speaking over breakfast Mary mentioned to Eddie that when she wakes up, she would have to ring Margi she'd love to tell her about the dream she's in. Eddie just looked at her and asked how she was going to contact Margi from the ship. "I'll use my mobile of course." Eddie looked more confused and asked her what a mobile was?

Mary scoffed at him and then said, that she'd forgot she was dreaming and people in the early 1950's wouldn't know what a mobile was. She'd have to wait until she woke up to tell him.

The Captain came by and asked Mary how she was enjoying her journey, she couldn't help noticing how the detail of her dream was so accurate. His uniform was the old black uniform from the fifties. She remembered seeing Captains and staff wearing when she went to the docks with Eddie's lunch, even down to the brass buttons and the badge on his cap. Everything was so realistic and so precise, she'd never had such a vivid dream.

She told the Captain she was enjoying the trip but looked forward to waking up from the dream she found herself in, so she could tell her sister about it, the Captain simply replied "you appear to be very awake to me Mrs. Jones, very awake indeed."

Having spent a few hours in what Mary thought was a dream state she decided to have a chat with a few of the people on board to see if maybe something they said would wake her. She wandered over to a young lady by the pool who she recognised from the next table the night before and introduced herself, to which the lady replied, "Yes I know who you are, we spoke last night, it's very nice to see you again, you look very refreshed this morning."

Starting to think maybe she was going a little bit mad, Mary asked if she had noticed anything different from the night before to which the lady said she didn't, although it was getting a little warmer as they sailed along to the coast of France.

This was now becoming a bit of a nightmare because she didn't seem to be waking, so she made her way to the bathroom and closed the door. Standing in front of the mirror she began pulling faces at herself, turned her back on the mirror and jumped in the air spinning around to face the mirror shouting at the top of her voice "BOO!." Nothing seemed to work. She began to dance around the bathroom pulling her own hair and singing out loud and then she stopped in horror. In the mirror was a very sheepish looking lady coming out of one of the cubicles. Mary turned to explain but the woman just screamed, held her hands over her face and ran like the wind out of the bathroom.

She decided to find Eddie and ask him to help her before she made more of an idiot of herself, so she headed for the top deck bar where she thought Eddie would be. She still couldn't believe the accuracy of her dream, ladies and gentlemen around the pool in their full costumes, with a few ladies daring to wear very short swimwear. Men playing shuffleboard in their wide kipper ties, double breasted suits and fedora style hats it was uncanny the reality of it.

"Eddie, I would like you to help me with a problem." "OK Mary, anything for you honey." Mary stopped in her tracks, he hadn't called her honey in years, at least 50 years, what the hell is going on!

The more she thought about it the more Mary was enjoying the fact that she was a youthful twenty year old again and decided to just go with the dream, enjoy the rest of the day and hopefully everything would be back to normal in the morning when she woke up. She resigned herself to a day of fifties entertainment.

There were ladies lined up sitting on chairs, they were using reels to wind in horses while people shouted for their horse to win. Her and Eddie had a flutter on which horse would win, she had number four and he had six.

"Come on number four" she shouted jumping up and down on her seat like she was the jockey, "Come on, giddy up."

Yessss! get in there, I won"

On the other side of the ship people were playing shuffleboard and deck tennis, it was a lovely atmosphere everywhere she looked.

Later that evening her and Eddie had a walk around the deck holding hands and stopped for a while to watch the ladies fancy dress hat competition, Mary thought to herself that she could easily have won that if she'd known it was on, she was always really good at making things and she could definitely have dreamed up a better hat than some of those.

They continued their walk and had a dance on the sun deck to the sound of the orchestra. It was just like the old days when they went to the dance hall, simply magical.

Going to bed that evening Mary was sorry that the day had to end but she knew that tomorrow would be back to normal and it was just nice to think she'd had a day of being young, even if it was only in her dreams.

CHAPTER FOUR:

Waking the next morning Mary hesitated before switching on the light, she didn't want the shock she'd had the day before.

She closed her eyes and switched on the light then slowly opened one eye and then the other. Once again, the room had changed it was brightly coloured with brightly coloured walls and multicoloured lamp shades with light teak furniture. She turned to see if Eddie was there and there he was, but it wasn't Eddie, or was it? he had a beard and long hair, 60's style hair. He was a bloody hippy.

"Oh my giddy aunt, what is going on, this can't still be in the same dream"

She jumped out of bed, ran to the bathroom and looked in the mirror. Once again, she let out an almighty scream. "THIS CAN-NOT BE HAPPENING!" Eddie sprung out of bed like a hippified gazelle and leapt across the room to see what had happened. "What's happening maaan?"

"What year is it?" she asked Eddie in a hesitant voice, "1965, why?"

"Because I'm standing here with Bouffant hair and it's dyed black, slightly different than when I went to bed, don't you think?"

"Errrr no, it looks lovely"

Mary just couldn't get her head around what was going on, she can't really be back in the 60's, it's just not possible and yet Eddie didn't seem to be in the slightest bit aware of any change. We can't have jumped ten years from yesterday never mind the fact that we're actually in our nineties and he's swanning around in his yellow Y fronts looking like George Harrison, what the bloody hell is happening?

Convincing herself that the dream had obviously continued she decided that, since she'd enjoyed herself so much the day before, she would go along with it and enjoy it while it lasted.

She went to the wardrobe and sure enough there were all her clothes from the 60's. "Well Eddie, since I look this good I think I'll wear a mini skirt, I always had good legs in my youth" Eddie looked at her with a smile on his face and said "Youth, what are you on about? you're only bloody thirty five, you're talking like you were eighty five."

Eddie got dressed and came through to the closet area where Mary was dressing, she took one look at him and immediately started to laugh, not a giggle but an uncontrollable laughter causing her to grunt between breaths. "What the hell have you got on?" Eddie was standing there adorned in a lilac and white paisley shirt with a collar you could ski down, brown corduroy bell bottom trousers and a pair of Cuban heel boots. Eddie seemed slightly offended "I think I look great; these are all the fashion." "Well this must be a dream, there's no way I'd have let you dress like that if I was awake, you look like a schoolteacher from Please Sir"!

Eddie, once again looked puzzled "Please sir? What's that? and why is it so bad?

Mary thought better of trying to explain and suggested heading on to the deck for a walk around and a cigarette.

Once on deck she couldn't help but notice how realistic the dream was, so much so that she could feel the burn of the cigarette on the back of her throat as she took a drag. The feel of the wind on her face and the sound of the sea rushing by, she could even taste the salt in the air. She didn't ever remember such vividness in any other dream she'd ever had. Maybe it was the gin and tonics she'd had or was it maybe something she'd ate that didn't agree with her.

In a sudden fleeting panicked moment Mary shouted out to Eddie, "Oh my giddy aunt, maybe I'm dead. They say you see your life flashing by when you kick it, I might be dying slowly, and I can see it all, there's no hope for me I can't speak to anyone to tell them! Fetch the doctor, he'll have to wake me up, so I can check I'm not dead"

The passengers sitting around her stared in astonishment at her sudden outburst and Eddie dropped his glass in shock. "What the friggin hell are you talking about, have you lost your mind woman, you're fine, we're on a ship in the middle of the ocean. You're far from dying, you're living it up"!

He sat her down and had one of the passengers bring her a glass of water before going to get the doctor. She sat there for a minute before carrying on with her outburst "If I'm not dying then this is the best prank I've ever seen and you lot are in on it, I'll bloody kill our Margi when I get home. She's played some tricks on me over the years but getting hundreds of people on a ship to join in is bloody ridiculous, it must have cost a fortune. Where's Jeremy Beadle?"

The lady sitting with her asked if that was her husband's name, and Mary started to cry, "No it isn't my husband, it's the fella who did Beadles About. You know, the prank program from the seventies or eighties." After blurting that out Mary realised that if it's the sixties in her dream, the lady wouldn't know who the hell Beadle was.

"Forget it, where's Eddie? My husband"

At this point the doctor arrived with Eddie and began to try to calm Mary down asking her what the problem was and why she was causing such a commotion. She asked the doctor what time it was, and he replied "11.15am Maam", she then asked what day it was to which he replied, "Tuesday Maam", ahh "yes but what date is it" she asked, "11th May Maam." Her next questions was the big one, the one she wanted to ask at the beginning but thought she'd build up to it. "okay okay, what year?" "1965 Maam" this was the answer Mary really didn't want to hear. She then proceeded to ask the doctor "Am I asleep or would you say I was awake?" "You are most definitely awake Maam"

"This cannot be happening, it's 2020 and I'm dreaming or dying, there's no other explanation for it"

"No Maam, it's definitely 1965 and you are definitely awake and alive, I wouldn't be a very good doctor if I didn't know if you were asleep or, even worse, if I didn't know if you were dead now would I?"

After calming her down enough to assure the other passengers that she would be alright, the doctor escorted Mary back to her room and gave her a couple of pills to calm her down before turning to Eddie and telling him to keep her out of the sun for a while just in case she's got a bit of sunstroke.

The doctor gave Mary a gentle tap on the shoulder and said that she would be fine after a few hours' sleep and that she should probably have a quiet afternoon to relax.

Mary lay on the bed contemplating her options, "do I pack up and get off the ship and find that I'm ninety again but in a foreign country, or do I enjoy my situation and stop worrying about how or why I'm here. After all, if I'm dreaming then it's the best dream I could imagine and if I'm dead, well, I'm dead, there's not a lot I can do about that."

Eddie waited until Mary had fallen asleep and decided to go up on deck for a couple of drinks, but as soon as he opened the door Mary sat bolt upright and said "where do you think you're going? I'm a young woman who needs to be taken out, where's the music and the dance floor, I'm not wasting this chance whether I'm actually here or not, I'm making the most of it."

With that she jumped up off the bed and ran to the wardrobe, "I'll have my gladrags on in a few minutes and we're going to enjoy ourselves." Eddie shrugged his shoulders and did exactly as he was told because, that's what he always did.

Making their way up to the deck, they stopped off for a bit of lunch in the Panama restaurant. As they entered Mary was busy looking at the food on everyone's tables, it all looked delicious. "Dead posh in here, best food I've ever seen, I hope I can dream it to taste as good as it looks", Eddie shook his head and found a table near the window.

Mary called the waiter and asked for the best steak on the menu with all the trimmings, and I might as well spoil myself with a glass of wine, or a nice cocktail. Eddie looked at her with a frown on his face and Mary said, "why've you got a face on ya like a bull-dog chewin a wasp?"

"Who do ya think you are love, Queen of bloody Sheba? You'd think we were made of money."

Mary thought for a few seconds and then told Eddie to shut up, and carried on with "Maybe I am, and she's having a great time so she's going to spoil herself as much as she can before she wakes up and finds she's back to being a ninety year old woman with an arse the size of Birkenhead, more wrinkles than an old washed out tenner and tits that flop on her knees when she sits down, with a wrinkly, old husband, with a forehead down the back of his neck, and a set of teeth from the dental superstore, living in a nowhere town on a crap pension and not only that but he should be thankful she's allowed him in her dream."

The couple on the next table were staring at them, open mouthed so Mary decided to carry on with her rant at them "What are you two gawping at? You two'll be old as well when I wake up and you'll both be in pensioners go carts with matching number bloody plates and England flags on the back. Mind ya flamin noses!"

The lady stood up uttering "Well I never!", Mary said "I'll put a pound to a piece of shite you did, you look the type!"

Once the couple had left Eddie placed his elbows on the table and cradled his face in both hands while shaking his head side to side. "What was that all about" he asked in a faint, almost defeated sounding voice.

"They deserved it, and besides I can say what I want in my own dream and the best part is, I don't have to apologise. Unless I said it out loud in my sleep, in which case, I apologise for calling you wrinkly and bald and I actually like where we live."

They both sat in complete silence throughout the meal with the odd glance between them to acknowledge how good the food was. Straight after they'd eaten, they had a few drinks and loosened up a bit, Eddie started to giggle about Mary's rant and the pair of them broke out into uncontrollable side-splitting laughter.

"I suppose they did deserve it a little bit, but I don't think I look that old" Eddie managed to get out between breaths.

They finished their drinks and made their way through the ship to where they could hear music. There was a fancy dress going on in the dance hall, so they decided to find a couple of seats and have a last drink before bed.

One of the fancy dress outfits reminded Mary of one she'd worn for her fortieth birthday when they had a house party. She was Gretel and Ed had been dressed up as Hansel. She grabbed Eddie's hand, gave it a squeeze and said "Dya remember that fancy dress party for my thirtieth birthday, I had a dress like that one?"

"I certainly do love, everyone thought I was a member of an Oompah band with my lederhosen, had to keep explaining the Hansel and Gretel thing, it was a great night though"

They finish their drink and head off to bed, tomorrow is their first stop in Palma, Majorca.

Getting into bed Mary was half hoping that tomorrow would be like the last few days, but she would kind of like to be back to old self. She's missed the peace and quiet of being old. But then if she's still young she can really enjoy Majorca with Ed.

Dream or no dream it's been fun.

CHAPTER FIVE:

The first words Mary heard the next morning were "Good morning love, wakey wakey, we're docked in Majorca. Are you getting up?"

Without opening her eyes, she immediately recognised Eddie's voice and smiled to herself, sounds like I've finally snapped out of it, that is definitely my Ed.

"What year is it Ed?"

"1978, love, why dya ask?"

Mary lets out a massive sigh and then turns over to go back to sleep, burying her face in the pillow and wrapping her arms around it to block out the world.

"Aren't you getting up, we're in Palma, we'll miss the tender to the dock, everyone is already up on deck waiting to go"

"Before I open my eyes, what are you wearing, and have you sorted your tatty head out? I'm not going through another day with you dressed like a schoolteacher from the sixties with a head like Axl Rose"

"I'm actually dressed very well, got my jeans and shirt on and who the hell is Axl Rose when he's about?"

She let out another sigh and sat up in bed, only to see Eddie in a pair of flares, the brightest shirt she'd ever seen and a rainbow coloured tank top. She burst out laughing and threw her face back into the pillow. "I hated the seventies, in the seventies, I hate them even more now! If you agree to change your gear I'll get up and go ashore"

After a bit of to-ing and fro-ing, Eddie finally agrees to change into something a little less bright. Mary gets up and goes to the bath-

room, looks in the mirror and, although not as shocked as previous days, she is still taken aback by the person looking back at her.
She shouts through the Eddie, "just checking, what year did you
say it was?"

"May 25th 1978 love"

She looks back in the mirror and utters under her breath; not too
bad for someone nearly fifty, I've had worse days.

"Come on love, we're gonna miss the boat!"

Mary goes to the wardrobe and as she expected there are all her
lovely clothes from the 70's. She chooses the shortest short dress
she can find, it's a lovely red and white chiffon and a pair of white
platform heeled sandals, finished her look off with a white hair-
band and a pair of hexagon shades before adding a bit of red lip-
stick and eyeliner. She has a quick check over in the mirror and
thinks to herself, bloody hell love you look awesome.

"Let's go Ed, the quicker we get through this the sooner I can get a
nice cuppa and a fag at home"

As she walks out Ed takes a long look up and down and tells her
that he might have changed his mind, maybe they should be a little bit late.

Mary gives a snigger and says, "you haven't looked at me like that
in twenty odd years, if it comes to that, it wasn't worth you looking at me like that for the last twenty odd years." She stops in her
tracks and thinks, wait a minute, maybe it is worth being a bit
late. "Turn that light off and get your kit off, you've pulled"

Lying in bed after the best sex she's had in three decades she starts
to think back to when they used to be like rabbits, couldn't keep
their hands off each other, back in the day. "Do you remember
when we used to have a proper sex life Ed? Back when you could
manage more than once in forty-eight hours without taking a
pill."

"I've never struggled with that love, and what's all that about twenty odd years, I was mustard in bed last week, in my opinion, you're getting proper forgetful. No idea what type of pill you might be on about but, unless they're for headaches, I've never needed one"

"I bet we've missed the boat now; it'll be a day on ship sitting around the pool on our own unless we hurry up."

They get dressed, grab their swimming gear and towels and rush down to the disembarkation deck to see if they can get off and they're in luck, there's a second tender.

Once ashore they look for a bus to take them to the beach and have to push their way on with Eddie holding on to Mary tightly to stop her falling back out through the doors. It's really hot and sweaty on the bus, no air conditioning and there's very little breeze through the open windows. People are so tightly packed on board that it's hard to breath. Mary can feel the breath of the woman behind her on the back of her neck and it's beginning to irritate her. Eddie holds her even tighter, less to do with her falling out of the door now and more to do with her falling out with the woman behind her.

Finally, they arrive at the beach, it seemed like hours, but in reality it was only twenty minutes. They get off the bus and head towards the white sandy beach down the beautifully paved footpath. Mary stepping onto the sand, instantly feels relaxed, soft and powder like between her toes, "It's like paradise" she says. Ed just smiles and nods before breaking into a jog towards a couple of sunbeds near the shoreline.

"Will these do love?"

"They'll do us just fine Ed, put the towels on em and we'll jump in that water"

It's the bluest water Mary has ever clapped eyes on with hardly a ripple, the closest she can compare it to is the sapphire in the ring she had at home, a ring that Eddie had bought her in Diggle's jewellers in town for her sixtieth birthday. The thought of that made her laugh to herself, I haven't even got it yet, I'm only forty-eight. How do I explain that one to Ed?

After a dip in the stunning blue waters, Ed and Mary spend a few hours lying in the warmth of the Mediterranean sunshine and reminiscing on their years together. Mary then has an idea. "I bet you we're still together in our nineties, and I can guess where we'll be living"

Ed replies with a shrug of his shoulders, "can't see me still being around at ninety, I'm falling apart now and I'm not even fifty"

"We'll have our own little bungalow in Huyton, a lovely one, with double glazing and central heating and a lovely garden with a little rose bed"

"Are you mad woman! We can't afford the rent on a tent, never mind our own house with stuff I've never even heard of"

Mary carries on with her prophecy, "You'll have a brand new car one day, and a really good job on the docks"

Eddie leans back in his deck chair and says "as mad as you are, it's a lovely dream to have. Come on we need to head back before we end up livin in Majorca"

Mary is not looking forward to getting on that bus again but it's the only way back so off they head to the bus stop.

It's not as packed heading back, most people have already gone so they manage to get a couple of seats. Mary sits by the window, it's dusty from the sand and dry heat but she watches with wide eyes as they pass the beautiful buildings and hotels along the way. She's enthralled by the mountains and how green everywhere is considering the temperatures. They point out the little houses and try to decide which one they'd have, if they could afford to, until they eventually arrive back at the port.

Back on the ship they find that the staff have laid on a buffet for the passengers on the deck. The choice of food is fabulous, every item looks like it's been specially made for each person, and the cakes are to die for. Cream cakes, chocolate cakes, there's even an anniversary cake for a couple of passengers who were celebrating twenty years together.

The anniversary cake gives Eddie an idea. It's Mary's birthday the following day and he wondered whether they'd make a cake to celebrate.

He makes an excuse to Mary and slips off to see the purser, to ask would they do it and the answer was more than he expected.

"We'll do more than that sir, we'll send the two of you a personal invite to the Captains cocktail party where we'll present the cake, followed by dinner at the Captains table. How does that sound?"

"Priceless, bloody priceless! She'll love it"

By the time Eddie gets back to the deck he sees Mary chatting with a couple, then he realises that it's the same couple she'd given abuse to in the restaurant the day before. Thinking that there could be a problem he sprints across the deck and grabs Mary by her arm saying, "walk away love, they're not worth it."

"Not worth what?"

"The argument"

"I'm not following you love, I'm having a nice conversation with this couple, David & Cheryl, are you losing it dear?"

"Errrrrr no! Don't you recognise them? They're the couple you had a go at in the restaurant yesterday"

"Of course I recognise them but they won't remember that it was over ten years ago!"

Eddie takes a step back, looks at the demeanour of the couple and must admit they don't seem to remember what happened the day before. Maybe he was mistaken, maybe it was a different couple. He takes a few deep breaths and begins a conversation with David. "Everything okay? enjoying your holiday?"

David gives a smile and raises his glass before answering "fan-bloody-tastic, lovely ship and great service, what more do you want"

Although a bit confused Eddie takes it that he must be mistaken and turns to Mary to apologise. Mary gives him a wry smile and a knowing wink and takes a sip of her drink.

After a walk on deck and waving goodbye to Palma they head off to their room for an early night. Mary thinks she might get lucky again and gives Ed a little pinch on the backside on the way back to the room. Ed knows she's going to get lucky again and speeds up the walk.

Before Mary goes to sleep, she says "Let's see what tomorrow brings."

CHAPTER SIX:

Mary wakes up to find herself alone in the room, she calls through to the bathroom to see if Eddie is still in the cabin, but there's no answer. She sits up in her bed and props her pillow up behind her, sitting back and folding her arms over the duvet. She sits there for a while just running the last few days through her head.

Day one, getting on to a cruise ship for the very first time, meeting some lovely people and the Captain, who was also lovely, having a few drinks during a very enjoyable sail away party and going to bed, all normal.

Day two, waking up in my twenties with a youthful body, lovely long hair, soft skin and a hunk of a hubby, who has the worst dress sense in the world. Then finding that I have all the clothes I loved when I was that age hanging in the wardrobe. Also making folks think I was a mental case by flipping out in the ladies loo. Not so normal!

Day three, waking up in my thirties, still having a great body, fantastic clothes in the wardrobe again, an even worse dressed hubby and making an absolute pillock out of myself to the ships doctor. Also, not normal!

Day four, expecting to wake up young, hoping to wake up old, actually woke up in my forties, there's a surprise, seems to be a pattern here. Wearing the best dress I've ever had and had the best sex I've had in years with my Ed. Went ashore in a beautiful place and visited the beach in Palma: had a lovely swim in the bluest sapphire sea I've ever seen before sunbathing on the whitest, white sand.

Day five, today is my birthday, just a guess, but I reckon I'm in my fifties and we're in the 1980's, seems logical after the past four days. I loved the clothes and the music from the eighties so it would be nice if this follows suit. Although, if I remember correctly, my fifties were when everything started to go south and my bingo wings began to give a little wobble. Far from normal, but it doesn't look like I'm getting out of this dream so I may as well enjoy it.

Eighties here I come, get the shoulder pads, head band and ra ra skirts out, or maybe not, probably won't look good on a fifty odd year old.

Mary decides it's time she made a move. Walking around the cabin singing "Happy Birthday To Me, and dancing to the sounds on the ship radio while searching through todays wardrobe for a lady's outfit fit for a semi-wrinkly, Mary is definitely getting in to the cruise life and beginning to really enjoy the dream she's stuck in all the more every day.

Just as she's getting ready to leave the cabin there's a gentle knock on the door and an envelope is pushed under with Mr & Mrs Jones written in very neat handwriting in gold ink. Very posh Mary thinks to herself before she opens it carefully trying her very best to not rip the posh envelope and takes out the contents.

It's a hand-written birthday card from the ships staff and an invitation for Eddie and her to attend the Captains cocktail party at 6pm followed by dinner at the Captains table at 7.30.

Wow! That is a wonderful surprise, and she's got nobody to tell. "Where the bloody hell is he anyway?"

When she's ready, she heads out onto the corridor to search for Eddie, with no idea where he might be.

Maybe he's gone to the ships shop to get her a present, or, knowing him, he forgot to get her a card and he's gone looking to see whether the shop has one.

She makes her way to the shops on deck six and on the way down she sees David and Cheryl, "Hows it goin? Have you seen Ed about?"

"No, sorry, he'll be about somewhere. See you later at the cocktail do"

Mary has a wonder around the shops, there's some very nice jewellery and lovely handbags, "Wonder if Ed's got me something from here? That'd be nice"

After a while of wandering around the shops and into the bar, she's ran out of ideas, only place left is maybe in the restaurant, so I'll have a walk down there.

As she enters the restaurant, the smell of baking and the sound of the chefs clinking and clanking with their knives and other utensils is quite intense; the main room is empty, so the smells and the noise are lingering in the air.

After a couple of minutes, she turns to leave just as Eddie walks out of the galley doors. "Where the friggin ell have you been? I've been lookin everywhere for ya"

Eddie looks very sheepish and is obviously searching for an answer. With a shaky voice he tells her he was helping to wash the dishes. "I haven't done a dish for over a week and I was missing it, so I asked if I could do a few"

"Do I look bloody stupid? You hate washing dishes; you'd sooner watch Everton than wash the dishes so don't give me that rubbish"

"Come on, what have you been up to?"

He thought as fast as he could, he couldn't tell her he was organising her cake for a cocktail party she knows nothing about, so he eventually came up with "on board cookery courses! They run them on the ship, so I booked you one for your birthday. It was going to be a surprise, but you caught me out."

"Aww, what a nice thought, except I hate cooking and you know it! Try again!"

Thoughts running through his head, shall I come clean, or should I try to blag her again?

"Wine tasting, you love wine, don't you? I didn't want to tell ya but you made me do it. I hope you're happy now that you spoiled the surprise"

Mary thought about it for a few seconds and then said "Sorry love, I shouldn't have pushed you, I'll really enjoy that, what kind of wine's is it?"

"Errrr red and errrr white, from abroad, it's dead posh and you'll have to wear something nice"

Eddie didn't lie to Mary very often, if he did it was with good intentions, hiding a surprise or if he knew she'd be upset over something, so she knew that it was probably rubbish but decided to accept it and move on. Although she had every intention of mentioning it at least once every hour to remind him that she was looking forward to the wine tasting and how much she loved him for making her birthday special. If he's telling the truth, it'll make him feel good and if he's lying it'll make him feel like shit. Either way it was a win, win for Mary.

Now that she'd found Ed they needed to decide what they were going to do for the day, there's games on different decks, quoits, a quiz and music by the pool, or there's bingo on in the bar, there's also a small cinema on board showing an old film.

Eddie decided the best option would be to go to the bar and Mary could play bingo, but Mary shot him down by reminding him that she was going wine tasting so it wouldn't be a good idea to drink before that.

Eddie thought about it and then said "How about we just find a couple of beds and relax, we might get a nice tan. I'll go back to the room and grab our towels and we could have a dip in the pool."

"That'll do nicely, build up a bit of a thirst for my wine tasting later. What time is it at by the way?"

"Six o'clock love"

"Oh right, where at?"

"It'll be in the restaurant, I should think"

Mary left him to stew for a few minutes before telling him that she'd had a birthday card off the staff with an invitation in it. "Apparently we're invited to the Captains cocktail party at six o'clock and it just happens to be in the restaurant." "How do you think they're going to fit the wine tasting in at the same time, in the same room?"

"Maybe I got the time wrong, it could be later"

"Ahh I see like 7.30 ish, do you think?"

"Yep, could be"

Once again, she let him think he'd got away with it for a couple of minutes before telling him that they were invited to dine at the Captains table at 7.30.

She handed him the envelope with the invitation in and told him she'd had it all day, he rolled his eyes and went the colour of a lobster, a lovely bright pink blush spread over his face, with the sweetest innocent look of a child caught in a lie on his face.

Mary smirked at him and told him to go and get the towels before she had to put him over her knee.

"Putting me over ya knee sounds like a better option to be honest"

She shook her head and told him to get the towels. "And don't forget the sun cream, we wouldn't want ya a permanent pink colour now would we"

They spent the rest of the afternoon sitting by the pool, listening to the music and having a bit of a sing along with a few of the other passengers. They had a couple of shandy's to quench the thirst before heading back to the room to get their gladrags on for the cocktail party.

Mary spent at least half an hour going through her wardrobe but, for the life of her, she couldn't choose which dress to wear.

The black sequined one, with the high heels, the red one with the white stilettoes or maybe the grey one with the silver shoes and the silver bag.

"Which one do I wear Ed, come on give me some help here"

"The black one, you'll look lovely in that"

"You're no use at all, I haven't got a bag to go with that"

"How am I supposed to know you ain't got a black bag? The grey one then"

"I prefer the red one to be honest, what do you reckon? You're not helping much here love"

"Dya know what Mary, the red one is lovely, and you really suit red. Wear that one, there ya go decision made"

"Mmmmm, don't you think it might be too bright for a cocktail party?"

"It's lovely, it goes with your hair. Wear the red one"

Eddie goes to the closet to get ready in his tuxedo and bow tie and ten minutes later he's all ready to go. He walks back into the bedroom and Mary is sitting there in the black dress. Eddie puts his hands to his face, shakes his head and mutters "I give up" under his breath.

He heads towards the door and asks whether she's ready.

"Hang on while I put me face on, it's not a five minute job making this kipper look good ya know"

Eddie starts to respond but stops himself just in time. "Ya look gorgeous love, come on, we're already late"

They make their way to the restaurant and on the way Mary gives him a little peck on the cheek. "Thanks for trying to cover up my birthday surprise, it was kinda cute, and by the way you smell lovely. Is that the aftershave I bought you last Christmas?"

"It's the one I bought me at Christmas, when you couldn't find it, but thanks for the compliment, you smell lovely too love."

They arrive at the doors to the restaurant and Eddie opens them up to allow Mary to go in.

She enters and is absolutely gobsmacked by how wonderful they've made the room look, it's like a fairy tale, the whole room is lit perfectly, and the tables are laid out fit for a king, or a queen. She can see through the crowd of people to the window and outside the sea is glistening with the light from the moon. "This is heaven Ed, I love it"

Eddie puts his arms around her and gives her a loving hug before turning to the chef and giving him a nod.

"HAPPY BIRTHDAY TO YOU, HAPPY BIRTHDAY TO YOU" rings out around the room and everyone is singing for Mary. The chef reacts to Eddies nod and brings out the most wonderful cake imaginable, layers and layers of beautiful white icing, topped off with an iced replica of the ship. She tries to keep herself in order, but a tear of happiness makes its way down her face and lands on the rim of her champagne glass. "Perfect, just perfect, thank you all so much"

She turns to Eddie and says "I told you I should have worn the red dress, can't believe I let you talk me out of it"

Eddie gives a huge sigh and replies "maybe I can talk you out of that one later eh love"

"Never mind the mucky talk, get me a slice of that cake, it looks delicious"

She takes a bite of the cake and it tastes as good as it looked with the softest sponge and absolutely perfect cream filling.

They have a cocktail and Mary sits down to take it all in. The Captain comes over and asks if he can have a seat next to her.

"How's your journey Mrs. Jones?"

Mary thinks back to that first night when the Captain said he hoped she had a good journey and she'd wondered what he meant at the time.

"You know, don't you?"

"Know what Maam?"

"You know about the time thing. You know how old I was when I came on board"

"No Maam, I know when you came on board you told me about how you'd like to relive some of your past, but you look exactly the same now as you did then"

Mary sat back in her chair and gave the Captain a doubtful look. "You must know, we all came on here as elderly passengers. Now we're middle aged at best"

Captain Thompson had a glimmer in his eye and a slight smile on his face but insisted that he had only seen all the passengers at the age they are today. "Maybe it's just a youthful feeling people get when they're enjoying themselves Maam. It's surprising what a bit of sun can do."

He stood up, leaned forward and took a hold of Mary's hand, bowed his head and gently kissed the back of her hand, before saying "enjoy the rest of the journey with your husband, these are the best years of our lives."

Eddie and Mary finished their drinks and headed through to dinner at the Captains table. On the way through they passed an open door heading out to the deck and Mary nipped out for a breath of fresh air, it had all been too much to take in and she needed a little break.

Staring out over the bow of the ship all she could see was the moon, which looked so much bigger than ever before and the stars, which seemed much brighter than ever before. The way they glistened off the sea, which looked black in the darkness of the night, it was incredible. This was truly a magical night and it was nowhere near over.

Mary walked back in and still had thoughts of the conversation with Captain Thompson on her mind, she would have liked to continue to question him about the trip and his comments, but despite her best efforts to sit near him, he was sitting too far away for them to converse over the table.

The dinner was absolutely stunning, the room was beautifully done with chandeliers hanging from the ceiling that looked like they'd been made from the purest of diamonds, the seats were made of the finest leather, tables were solid oak with a beautiful shine and the food was incredible. Maybe it was the wine and the champagne but there seemed to be a haze in the air that made it so calming and gave it an air of finery and elegance.

It was a night to remember for ever.

After dinner and an Irish coffee, or two, the Captain thanked everyone for attending, told them all how much he'd enjoyed their company but made his apologies and said he had to leave, he had an early start the next day because they were docking in Rhodes.

As Mary and Eddie made their way back through the corridors of the ship Mary asked Eddie whether he had enjoyed the trip so far and whether he'd noticed anything different on each day of the cruise.

He thought about for a while and then told her that it was probably the best time they'd shared together and that he loved her more now, in this moment, than he had ever loved her. She was his world and he would be lost without her in it.

They stopped walking to hold each other tight and kissed like they had just met that night.

"I love you Ed. Thank you so much for the best night of my life, it was beautiful."

CHAPTER SEVEN:

Mary wakes to the sound of the alarm at the side of the bed. It's the first time they've set an alarm since they've been on the ship but they're both really looking forward to seeing Rhodes.

She rubs her eyes and begins to wonder what today will bring, she turns over and sees the back of Eddies head on the pillow, his hair is beginning to thin and it has hints of silver grey, although it is still there so she knows she still isn't out of the dream she seems to have been in for ages. Going by previous days it must be 1990s

"Eddie, what year is it?"

"EDDIE!"

Mumbling Eddie says "1997"

"Thought so, is it May by any chance?"

"Yep"

Eddie starts to snore again, so Mary gives him a poke in the back

"Oy, Wake up Ed, we'll get some brekky before we go ashore"

Eddie turned to face her, and she reeled back in disgust.

"What's up with you woman?"

"What's up with me? You've got a walrus moustache stuck on ya top lip like a feckin big hairy slug and you're asking what's up wi me. Get that off or I'm divorcing ya!"

"It's been there for weeks and you haven't said a word"

"Get it off or you'll be visiting Rhodes on your own, I'm not walking around with Willy the walrus all friggin day"

Eddie goes to the bathroom and checks himself out in the mirror. "I think I suit it, what's wrong with it?"

"Listen Willy, if that doesn't come off, I'll be leaving you and if you think I'll be kissing ya, you've got another thing comin"

He looks in the mirror again and he's determined that it's staying on, mumbling to himself and telling himself that he's a grown man, he'll keep it if he wants, and there's nothing she can do about it.

"Is that thing off yet?"

"Yes love, it's all gone"

"Good"

With that she jumps up and starts singing and dancing "Where's ya Willy gone, where's ya Willy gone!", which Eddie doesn't find funny in the slightest.

Mary goes into the bathroom and catches a glimpse of herself in the mirror, she's starting to look old again. Sixty seven, she can claim her pension and her bus pass again even if she went home today.

It takes her a bit longer to get ready today, she's got bits that are aching that didn't ache the day before, knee joints, elbows and shoulders feel a lot weaker. She gets herself ready and the two of them head out into the corridor to go to the restaurant for a hearty breakfast before heading out.

They get to the stairs and both of them stop staring up the first flight, neither of them fancy the climb.

"Shall we take the lift love?"

"Great idea Mary, I was just going to suggest that myself to save ya legs, although I could get up the stairs if I wanted to, but I'll go with you, so you're not lonely"

The lift doors open and there's a gentleman in there with his wife in a wheelchair. Eddie looks at the fella and asks him are they having a nice holiday, the man nods and says that it's hard getting around the ship pushing a wheelchair, but he's still enjoying the break in the sunshine.

"Goin up or down?"

"Up please, off to the restaurant and then off out to see Rhodes Town and the Acropolis at Lindos"

The man gives him a questioning look "You two gonna walk up there?"

"Nah, we'll get on one of the donkeys, too bloody old for that hill"

Mary gives Eddie a little slap on the back of his head "I'm not sitting on one of them donkeys, it's bloody cruel. If we can't get up on ar own steam we're not going up"

They arrive at the restaurant, which is quite empty considering it's a shore day, there's usually lots of people rushing around to get their breakfast before they go ashore. Maybe some have already gone or are going later.

Following another lovely breakfast, Mary and Eddie grab their bag and make their way down to disembark. There's quite a few in the lift, many with silver hair and Mary notices the walking sticks are starting to mount up.

Mary is realising that she and Eddie are getting old. Late sixties isn't too old but it's definitely a different age than she felt yesterday and it's definitely showing on Ed.

They leave the ship and make their way to the bus for the first part of their journey into Rhodes Town. On the way they pass little churches painted white with lovely blue doors and blue steeples, some of them wouldn't hold more than ten people.

"They're gorgeous, they look like little Christmas cakes" Mary remarked

Once they arrive in Rhodes town, they realise how hot it is, it's over ninety degrees and the humidity is stifling, there doesn't seem to be any shaded areas anywhere where they can cool off.

They decide to have a little walk through the streets, where there is at least a bit of shade from the searing heat of the sun. The old cobbled streets lead off the main square and are filled with souvenir shops and small bars and restaurants.

The old stone faced buildings are a sight to behold, they have brown and golden colour blocks making up the ancient façade and beneath, in total contrast, is the bustling of the holiday makers in their brightly coloured clothing, swirling in and out of the shops, picking up their miniature Colossus statues and pretty fridge magnets, while the sound of Greek music from the centre of the square is partially drowned out by the chitter chatter of the hundreds of people and of the children playing in the fountain.

Mary and Eddie look around for a while and Mary buys a fridge magnet with a lovely picture of the harbour for Margi. "She'll love that on the fridge, it'll make her think of us."

They have a look in a few more shops and then choose a little café bar with a parasol and a view of the old castle and sit down for a cup of tea and a bite to eat.

Eddie asks the waiter for a menu and two cups of English tea.

"Far cry from when we used to be bevying from lunch time onward eh love"

"Yep, sooner have a cuppa and a biscuit now, dya think we're getting old?"

"You might be, I can still bevy wi the best of em"

Mary laughs and tells Ed to have a pint if he wants, he'll probably enjoy it and it'll cool him down in the heat.

"Nah, I'll stick with my cuppa, hot drinks help to cool ya down"

"That's nonsense, how can a hot drink cool ya down"

"Brings your inner temperature up to the outside temp, so makes you feel cooler, it's a scientific fact"

Mary gives him a look of distain and shakes her head, then proceeds to drink her hot drink.

They sit in the little café for a while, watching the world go by while holding hands. Eddie gives Mary's hand a squeeze and asks if they're going to bother with Lindos. Mary says "not unless we can hike up there on our own two feet, I refuse to get on one of them poor donkeys. They're out there in the red hot sun all day, don't even know whether they get water breaks."

"Well I'd probably make it up there, but you'd struggle so we'd best leave it eh?"

With a knowing smile, Mary agrees and tells Eddie to get them another cuppa while they make plans for the afternoon and evening when they get back onto the ship.

It's a beautiful day and they're both spending it with the person who means the most in the world to them in a beautiful place and wonderful sunshine, how much better could life get?

After their cuppa, Mary gathers her things together and asks Eddie if he's ready to head back to the ship, if they get back early enough, they can get a couple of chairs by the pool and have a quiet read.

They head back and the whole way there they link arms, "not bad for two old pensioners eh kid" Mary says to Eddie.

"Not bad at all love, like two peas in a pod"

They get back to the ship and find a quiet spot on the starboard side so they can watch the sun go down over the Aegean.

Sitting with their chairs pulled together and a blanket over their knees, they watch as the orange, pink, purple and red sky lights the horizon. The sun sitting in between the low clouds and reflecting off the calm sea. It's a sight that you could never tire of seeing.

Eddie pipes up "It's like a painting, Gods very own canvas and it's all yours, he painted it for you, and I showed him how."

"Shut up ya silly old sod, you can't paint, I remember you once tried to paint the bloody living room and ended up with more on the carpet than was on the bloody wall"

They sit there until the sun has gone down and the temperature starts to drop and then make their way back to their room to get changed for their evening meal.

Back at the room they put a bit of music on and have a little sing along while they get ready to go out.

"Dya know what Ed, tonight we should party like it's 1999. Let's kick our shoes off and dance our socks off till we drop, it'll do us good"

"I'm up for that, how about we have a glass or two of wine with our tea and then hit the dance floor, Lets show these old fogies how to stay young"

"Come on then Mary. Are we still taking the lift? Them feckin stairs will be the finish of me"

Going to the restaurant, holding hands with a renewed spring in their step Ed and Mary were happy as Larry.

Eddie found them a seat in the restaurant and shouted out in his best posh voice "Excuse me waiter, could I have a bottle of house white please, two glasses and don't spare the horses"

"I've got a feeling this might be a night to remember love, I'm feeling sound as a bloody pound, you might even get lucky later, depending on the strength of this wine"

"Bloody hell Ed, you were like a ninetyten year old earlier today trying to walk on them cobbles in the town, what have you been on?"

"I've watched the sun set on another day in our lives and I've been fed on the love of a beautiful woman, I'm ready for anything"

"If ya not careful, you'll be ready for the knackers yard, ya soft get"

They have their meal and polish off a bottle and a half of wine between them before heading for the bright lights of the dance hall. When they get in there, they swirl around the dance floor like two love struck teenagers with itchy feet.

Round and round they go without a care in the world, until they eventually wear themselves out and plonk themselves down on a couple of seats to watch the Dad dancing and the Mum moves before heading off to bed, giggling like giddy kids.

Mary has obviously realised that tomorrow won't just be another day, but another decade and although Eddie doesn't know it, tonight was probably their last bounce around a dance floor. This saddens her for a while, but in the back of her mind she knows at some point they're going to be ninety year olds again, she can't dream forever.

She says goodnight and kisses his forehead as he drops into a deep sleep.

She's praying that tomorrow doesn't come, all the fun, laughter and love she's seen over the last seven days has been fantastic and tomorrow is the next to last day of their trip.

Trying her very best not to fall asleep, but it's inevitable, she eventually does.

CHAPTER EIGHT:

3.30am Mary wakes up needing to use the bathroom, she gets up as quietly as possible to avoid waking Eddie. It's the first time she's woken up in the night, so she's a bit curious.

She makes her way to the bathroom but on the way she hesitates, thoughts start to rush through her head, have I actually woken up from the dream, will I still be in the 1990's or will I have moved on to 2000's? Surely she wouldn't have woken up to go to the loo in a dream? Or would she?

Finally getting to the bathroom she stops to check in the mirror, I look the same as when I went to bed, must still be 1997? Then again how much would I change if it was in 2000's, might only be 2001, wouldn't change that much in four years.

"Ahh sod it, I'll have a pee and worry about it tomorrow." Suddenly panic sets in, she says to herself in the mirror "I remember doing this as a kid, I really hope I'm not going to pee the bloody bed, size of me now it'll wash Ed out the bed, he'll be floating down the crack at the side of the bed."

She swills her face to make sure that she's awake and then goes to the toilet. On her way back to she lifts the duvet and checks the bedding, "bone dry, panic over."

Once she's back in bed she lies there for a bit with a thousand thoughts running around her head. Rhodes was fantastic and what a night they had when they got back on board, it was an amazing day. In a couple of hours, she'll know whether she's in her seventies or back to her normal old self.

She's racking her brains to remember what she looked like in her seventies, did she have grey hair, or did it still have some colour, was she wrinkled or still looking youthful, she couldn't for the life of her remember.

The next thing she hears is Eddie saying, "Come on love it's nearly arf nine, are we making a move? Gonna miss the last day of sun"

"Does it matter, tomorrow we'll be back to the repetitive daily shit, I'll be ninety, you'll be ninety one and it'll be get up, get dressed, you get the mornin paper and I get me cuppa and a piece of toast. We sit watching mornin tele till our brains are numb and then we have a crap microwave dinner. Maybe we'll get a visit off are Marg, if we're lucky, but other than that, from two o'clock onward we'll just be waiting to go to bed again, what kind of life is that?"

"Bloody hell Mary, something I said? I only asked if you was getting up"

"Sorry love, just a bit pee'd off cos this is nearly over, it'd be lovely to just stay on here and not go back to our normal everyday lives wouldn't it"

Eddie sat on the edge of the bed and, in a quiet, almost mousey, voice, he said "Mary? Do you regret anything in our lives together? I've tried my very best to be the best husband I could, but sometimes I feel like you're not happy and it's my fault. I've always done my best for us, but maybe it wasn't enough."

Mary sitting up in bed, puts her arms around Eddie "Ed, sorry for what I just said, it wasn't a dig at you, we've had a lovely life together and you've been the perfect husband, the best I could have wished for. I'm just a bit down cos this holiday will be over tomorrow"

They give each other a hug and Mary pats Eddie on the shoulder before Eddie says, "You're only seventy eight you know love, a long way off ninety that, although I feel ninety one today, bloody aching all over."

Mary makes the effort to get out of bed and realises what Eddie has just said. "2008 is it love?"

"It certainly is, who'd have thought we'd have lasted this long?"

"Well I reckon we've got a good ten years at least left love, if it comes to that I'll guarantee it"

Eddie gives a little laugh and says, "it'd be great to think we have, but I seriously doubt it, I never thought I'd make it to the next century never mind eight years into it. Never thought I'd see mobile phones and computers and things that can record stuff off the tele, don't think it's anything I'll ever get used to using but they are great. Imagine what they'll have in ten years if we are still around."

Mary says, with a grin on her face "They'll probably have machines you can talk to in your own living room and ask em questions like what's the weather today and tell me the news, or what's the capital of Sweden and they'll have all the answers, wouldn't that be amazin."

"It'd be scary, a machine that knows more than humans, that's some weird thinking that love, you should write to someone about that."

Mary gets herself ready and the two of them step out into the corridor. It's a fair walk to the lifts and Mary notices how much longer it's taking them to get there today. They get into the lift and Eddie is looking at the buttons, moving his head backwards and forwards and squinting his eyes. "Oh bloody hell, I've left me specs in the room, I'll shoot back and get them."

As soon as he's gone Mary sits down on the stairs to wait for him and start to weep, not a full cry but a saddened weep. We really are getting old she thinks, by tomorrow I'm going to need my specs too.

Eddie comes back with his glasses and wearing a flat cap, "Why have you got that on love, it's still warm, you won't need that until we get home."

"I feel the cold on my head so I'd sooner wear it, ya lose ninety percent of ya heat through ya head ya know"

They enter the lift and Mary says, "nothing to do wid ya losing ya hair then?"

"I haven't lost me hair; I know exactly where it is. It's in a pile on my pillow"

Mary lets out a loud laugh and gives Eddie a peck on the cheek. "You may be getting old but ya not losing ya mind lad."

Mary didn't fancy breakfast, she said she'd eat a bit later so Eddie went to get his on his own. While he was sitting in the restaurant a lady came over and asked if he minded that she sat down because all the other tables were full, or people had claimed them by putting bags and towels down.

Eddie told her it was no problem; he was only having a few bits and then he'd be done.

The lady went off to get her food and asked if Eddie wanted a cuppa while she was up, he told her he was going to get one on his way out for himself and his wife.

The lady came back and sat down, Eddie asked how her trip has been and she paused for a minute before telling him that it was going great until they'd visited Rhodes. Her husband had fallen over while they were out and hit his head on the cobbles. He'd been taken to hospital and checked over and they said he was fine, but he woke up this morning with terrible pain in his side, apparently when he fell, he'd broken his ribs.

She then explained that they'd had to travel from Nottingham to Liverpool to catch the ship and she had no idea how her and her husband could get off the ship with all their luggage and get a train back to Nottingham when he could hardly get out of bed never mind carry luggage.

Eddie asked her how old her husband was and if they could get any help off their family or friends.

"He's eighty three and already has heart problems, is there any way you could help us or do you know where I could get help?"

"Errrrm, I don't drive now, too bloody old, I can ask whether Marg would take you, but I'd have to speak to Mary, my missus to see if that's alright."

Eddie stands up and heads out to see Mary thinking, why did I ask her how her trip was, now I've got to sort all her problems out or I'll look a right pillock.

He finds Mary in a little corner by the pool and explains what had gone on over breakfast. "What do I do now, dya think Margi will take em to Nottingham when we dock?"

Mary gives it a little thought and tells Eddie to stop worrying, it'll sort itself out by tomorrow. She obviously knows that tomorrow will be years later and any injuries the old man has now will be gone by then, but she can't say that to Eddie. She'd had enough problems in the first few days trying to explain to people that she was in a series of Quantum Leap but without Sam Beckett and Al to back her up.

Eddie moves around the corner hoping to hide himself away in case the lady passes and sees him. "I really don't know what to tell her love, she's probably relying on me to sort it out now."

"Ed, just tell her you'll sort it all out and we'll speak to ar Marg tonight to see if she'll do it"

"Dya think she will?"

"Will what?"

"Take em to Nottingham, ya know, if I tell the lady that Margi'll take them, dya think she will?"

After a moment of thought, Mary just tells him she will, one hundred percent. Then tells him to stop panicking and sends him off to get the cuppa that he'd obviously forgot to bring back from the restaurant.

Eddie goes back to get the tea hoping that he doesn't bump into the lady. He pulls his cap down to the top of his eyebrows and bends his head slightly to one side to try to hide his face from people walking by. After making four cups of tea he heads back to

Mary with a tray.

Mary asks "why've ya brought four?"

"Save me another trip, and I had a bit of a thirst, so I got two each."

"You're scared to go back ain't ya, in case that woman collars ya."

"No"

"Why are ya hidin ya face then?" Walkin round like inspector Clouseau, ya muppet"

"I don't wanna burn my head, and I had something in my eye"

"Come on Ed, we'll move to another deck so you can sunbathe in peace, bring the towels"

They gather their things and make their way up to one of the upper decks where hardly anyone goes because there's no shade and the waiters rarely go up there. All the way Eddie is doing his Inspector Clouseau impression and using the towel to hide his face.

After a few hours relaxing in the sunshine a voice breaks up the silence, "Mr and Mrs Jones are you enjoying yourselves." Mary opens her eyes and there's a blurred figure dressed in white standing over her. "Oh my god! I've defo kicked the bucket this time. Are you Jesus?"

"Well not quite Maam, I'm the Captain, but thank you for the promotion"

Mary's eyes start to clear and she moves slightly sideways to remove the sun from directly behind the figures head. "Ahh, now I see you, scared me there for a minute, thought you'd come to collect."

The Captain asks if he's okay to join them for a few minutes. "just one minute I'll clear the next bed so you can sit down"

Mary shifts the sun cream and her bag off the bed and the Captain takes a seat.

"Beautiful day Mrs Jones"

"It certainly is Captain, errr, what do we owe the pleasure?"

The Captain begins by saying how on the last day he liked to have a wander around the ship and have a chat with the passengers, he liked to ask how they'd enjoyed their journey with Twilight Cruises and if the trip had been what they'd wished for. He went on to say that, although he'd captained a number of these trips, that this was possibly his favourite and that seeing the love between her and Ed was a beautiful thing.

Mary stared straight at him, started to speak but stopped herself before checking over her shoulder to where Eddie was lying to see if he was awake, which he obviously wasn't, he rarely snored when he was awake.

"You know what I've been through on here don't you?"

"You asked me the same question a few nights ago Mrs Jones, and I answered you truthfully then. You are exactly the same age that I saw when you arrived on the ship. Your age is not what has changed during your journey, but what has changed is your memories, forgotten memories have returned, hidden memories that you had locked away in the furthest reaches of your mind have been brought to the front. Do you not remember dancing the night away with your husband back in 1997, it wasn't on a ship, it was in a dance hall in Liverpool, but it was a fantastic night that you revived the memory of on the Twilight."

Mary suddenly started to think back, "Oh my giddy Aunt, I do remember it, we danced all night until we couldn't dance any more. I remember my birthday party, when he got me the cake and surprised me with al of my friends in our local and everyone sang happy birthday when I walked in. It's all coming back, but why am I remembering, and Eddie is oblivious to it all?"

The Captain stands up and says, "I can't tell you why it's you and not Mr Jones, I honestly have no idea. Maybe it's your job to remind him and to give him those memories back. I'm just here to help bring them back for you to do with whatever you wish.

The Captain walks away and leaves Mary pondering what has happened over the past week. Everything that has happened on the ship is an old memory, they've just been brought back brighter and more colourful than before.

The couple of hours in the café in Rhodes holding hands and chatting about what they should do next, could have been any afternoon in a tearoom in Llandudno, which at the time were golden memories but they're not memories that she ever thought of, never discussed them with Ed. Maybe it's time she did.

Mary spends a while going through the week's events, each day was a brilliant day, and each day had a comparable memory throughout their lives together.

Was this a dream, or did they really find themselves on a journey through their years together. She wonders how she is going to explain it all to Eddie, how do I go through it all with him without making a complete fool out of myself.

Mary lays back in her sunbed and begins to put all the pieces together in her mind before she tells Eddie, but eventually comes to the conclusion that it would be better to tell him when they are home and she's had time to digest it all herself.

She wakes Eddie up and they pack up their belongings before heading back down to the pool area.

They order themselves a glass of wine and pull a couple of chairs together by the bar.

"Well Ed, what's this trip been like for you love? Has it maybe brought back a few memories?"

"It hasn't really brought memories back, but it's defo made some, it's been brilliant"

"Well maybe we can go through all our old photos when we get home, see what we can find in there"

"Yeah, I'd like that, it's been ages since we dragged them out of the loft"

They spend an hour at the bar chatting and discussing what they'd like to do next, they've done caravanning, most of the UK in hotels and now they've been cruising.

"What about parachuting love, you'd look great in one of those suits they wear and the silly little helmet, like that's gonna save ya life from thirty thousand feet!

"I think we're a bit old for that now Ed, maybe something with both feet on the ground"

It's getting to late afternoon so they decide to go back to their room and order room service for their last night, but instead of just ordering anything Mary suggests they order something they've loved over the years, so they carefully go through the menu picking out food until they find it. "Fish, chips and mushy peas never thought they'd do that on a ship Mary."

"Well let's order that an ask em do they do doorstop bread n butter, be like home from home"

They call through, place their order and settle down ready for the treat. "Remember when ya used to get em wrapped in the Echo, always tasted better in newspaper than they do now. The salt n vinegar used to soak into the paper and the print'd come off on ya hands"

"Yeah love, them were the days, all too clinical now wit the polystyrene boxes, ya only get half the chips in them that ya used to in the Echo."

Finally, their food arrives, fish, chips and mushy peas and a bottle of wine. They dig in and polish the whole lot off, not even a crispy chip left on the plates.

"Bloody delicious Mary, best meal we've had all holiday, what dya reckon?"

"It's up there with the steak you moaned about, if not maybe a bit better"

"Well Ed, this is our last night, we could go out and watch the show or we could have an early night and a bit of a cuddle, I'll leave it up to you"

"I reckon we go an get pissed"

"Okay, if that's your choice, I'll go along with it"

"Nah, I'm only messin, early night and a cuddle sound brilliant"

With that they get themselves changed and get into bed, knowing that tomorrow will be the last day on ship.

After a short while Eddie begins to nod off and leaves Mary in deep thought. She is really looking forward to getting home now, getting the old photographs out and going through the old albums. She still has all their old cards from their wedding, old Christmas and birthday cards, copies of awards Eddie got from work over the years. She couldn't wait to get home to rummage through them all.

A trip down memory lane.

CHAPTER NINE:

Mary didn't sleep too well, probably due to the excitement of seeing Margi and being able to tell her all about the trip and do her best to explain the whole thing. She's not too sure how to explain it but she was going to do her best.

She checked her watch on the side of the bed and it was 6.30, a bit earlier than she meant to get up, but she'd be home by tonight and she can have as much sleep as she wanted then.

She got out of bed and looked across to Eddie. He had a thin strand of grey hair around the back of his head and she knew they were back to their normal age, which she had expected to be fair, so it wasn't any shock.

"EDDIE, get up lad, we'll be back in Liverpool this afternoon, gorra pack and get some brekky."

Eddie gave a little glance over his shoulder and muttered through his gummy mouth, "Good mornin sexy, where've ya bin all me life?"

"Ask me again when you've got ya teeth in ya silly old sod, come on get yer arse in gear, we've got to pack"

Eddie rolls out of bed and starts to walk across the room, Mary looks at him "Bloody hell Ed, you've got more wrinkles than nelly the friggin elephant, it's like looking at the skin on a rice puddin all brown and cracked"

"Have ya looked in the mirror lately love? I thought you hadn't ironed ya nighty till I noticed ya haven't got one on"

They have a laugh, but they both know that their skin no longer fits its bits.

Mary is getting her stuff together and is singing her little head off,

Eddie comes back through and asks what she's so happy about. "Today is the first day of the rest of our lives Ed, we'll be back in ar little house, in ar own bed with ar own knives and forks, and on top of that I get to see ar Margi"

"Whoop de bloody do! All that stuff and we get to see Margi, I'm over the bloody moon"

They spend an hour or so getting their bags packed and Mary insists on cleaning around before they leave even though there's a cleaner coming in as soon as they leave. "Better that the cleaner thinks we're clean love, wouldn't want em thinkin we're scruffs."

After the cleaning is done, they make their way down the corridor to go for their last breakfast on the ship.

If there's one thing they can't moan about it's the food, absolutely fantastic, every single meal was perfect but especially their fish and chips on their last night.

Sitting down for breakfast they see a couple and Eddie thinks he recognises the lady, "do ya know who that is love? Sure I've spoke to her before"

Mary looks and sees the lady who Eddie had been avoiding the day before but now years older, she's with her husband who looks to be in fine fettle, as she knew he would be.

"Probably someone you've seen around the ship love, just eat ya brekky."

Just as they're leaving the table Mary sees Captain Thompson in the doorway, she tells Edie that she'll be back soon and makes her way towards him, when she gets to the doorway the Captain greets her with "Good morning Maam, how are you this fine morning?"

"All the better for meeting you sir, the whole journey has been special, you have given me so much to look forward to and to look back on. Thank you, Captain Kenneth P Thompson, I will never forget you."

The Captain once again took her hand, bowed his head and gave Mary a gentle kiss on the back of her hand. "Memories are a very precious commodity Mrs Jones, cherish them always.

With that he turned and walked away, and Mary knew that was the last time she would see him.

She made her way back to the table and got hold of Eddies hand, "come on love, let's have a last look around the ship, we'll be in Liverpool in a couple of hours."

They walk along the lido deck past the pool and the bar and make their way up to deck sixteen where they have a clear view of the land in the distance.

Eddie pulls out a seat for Mary to sit and watch as they make their way around the tip of Anglesey and head towards the Mersey.

While they're sitting there they pull their chairs together, put a blanket over their knees and hold hands, knowing that they'll soon be home.

There's still an hour or so before they arrive so Mary tells Eddie that, since she's been up early, she'll have a short nap and then gently nods off helped by the gentle rocking of the ship.

CHAPTER TEN:

Mary wakes up to the sound of the ships horn, giving a long blast, but as she opens her eyes, she quickly realises that she's in a strange room, with very bright lights and strange sounds. Looking down she sees Eddies hand in hers, as it was when she fell asleep, but it has a tag on and he has a catheter in the back with tubes in.

She closes her eyes and squeezes them tightly shut before reopening them, but nothing has changed. She looks around the room. Is it a hospital ward or a nursing home, did he take ill and they're in the ship's hospital, she has no idea what happened between the ship and where she is now?

She gently releases Eddies hand and gets to her feet, "Where the hell is this?" she says out loud.

Mary makes her way to the door and steps out. "Hello, is there anybody here!"

"HELLO, ANYBODY!"

A woman dressed in a blue and green uniform comes out of a room and walks up to Mary. "Hello Mrs. Jones, I hope you slept well, how's your husband? I'll be in shortly to check everything is okay."

Mary is totally taken aback by the calmness of the nurse. "Who are you, where is this and why is my Eddie in that bed?"

The nurse tells Mary that they are in a ward for Alzheimer's sufferers and that Eddie had been in there for over a week, he was brought in after a car accident on the way to Liverpool to join a cruise. The accident left him unconscious and Mary with a head injury, which she'd recovered from much faster than expected.

"That's not possible, we went on the cruise, we had a wonderful time and we were just getting back today."

The nurse carried on telling Mary that Eddie had obviously had a slow onset of Alzheimer's prior to the head injury but the traumatic impact has caused a rapid onset. The best Mary could do would be to sit with him and talk to him, keep his mind active, maybe run through some memories that may help him to remember who she is.

"What dya mean, remember who I am, course he remembers, I'm his bloody wife, how would he forget that"

"Sometimes it's good to use photographs and other memorabilia as a stimulus to bring back memories or songs you used to sing. Some people respond really well to songs and others respond to tangible things like photos or things they can see and touch."

Mary goes back into the room and Eddie is awake, she walks over to his bed and says, "How ya feelin Ed?"

He looks at her like he's never seen her before in his life, "Is Terry here? I wanna see Terry, he's got things for me."

Terry was Eddies older brother who had passed away in the war in 1944, he'd never mentioned him in all these years, but thought he was there now.

Mary tried again "Ed, it's me Mary, your wife"

"Where's Terry, why are you in my room, I want to see Terry"

Mary starts to cry uncontrollably and begs Eddie to look at her, "you must remember me, we've been married for 68 years, you must remember that"

"I'd like you to leave now please, Terry will be here soon"

"TERRY IS DEAD, he isn't coming here, he's gone"

Hearing the conversation, the nurse asks Mary to come with her while she calms down. She makes Mary a cup of tea and sits down with her in a small room.

"I know it's hard, but there's a likelihood that he may never remember who you are, all you can do is try to jolt his memory. Do you have anything you can bring with you? Something that might set off a memory in his mind"

Mary looks at the nurses name tag, Carol P Thompson, she suddenly realises that the whole trip was a dream, it was a way for her to come to terms with Eddies state of mind and those memories were the memories she had of their lives together.

"I'll call Margi and get her to bring the boxes from the loft, she'll know what to bring"

The nurse drops her head and goes silent, she then raises her eyes, without raising her head, to look at Mary and asks her if Margi was driving the car?

The look from the nurse was enough to tell Mary that it was bad news.

Mary breaks down, drops to her knees on the floor and lets out a deathly scream.

"Noooooo! Not our Margi, please tell me she's okay. Please, please God, tell me she's alright"

"I'm so sorry Mrs Jones, Margi passed away at the scene, the paramedics did everything they could, but they couldn't save her"

Inconsolable, Mary crawls into the corner of the room and puts her arms around herself tightly, rocking to and fro she blubbers out through her tears "My little sister. Why?"

The nurse asks Mary if she can contact anyone else to come and sit with her?

"There is nobody else, my sister and my husband, that's it. What do I do now, I'm alone and my husband doesn't even know who I am?"

CHAPTER ELEVEN:

Three months of visiting Eddie every day is beginning to take its toll on Mary, she is sitting at home and contemplating whether to give up, she's been to see him every single day and no matter what she said or did, he still has no idea who she is, every day she leaves the nursing home and spends the whole night crying into her pillow.

The only person he asks for is Terry, it's a daily heartbreak for Mary when Eddie asks her when Terry is coming to see him and she has to keep telling him, he'll be there tomorrow.

She drags her frail body up out of the chair and forces herself to go to the nursing home, she has to get a bus there and the driver has gotten to know her over the last few months.

"Good morning Mary, off to see him again?"

"Yes love, maybe today he'll say it, maybe today he'll say my name"

"Why do you do it to yourself Mary, going there everyday and knowing that he hasn't got a clue who you are or any memory of your times together?"

"You're right he has no idea who I am or any memory of our lives together, but I know who he is, and I remember our whole sixty eight years, I go to see him because I remember"

Mary arrives at the nursing home and enters the ward, "Good morning Carol, how's he been since yesterday?"

"he's been sound, still waiting for Terry to arrive, but other than that he's sound"

Mary walks into Eddies room and he turns to look at her as she walks in. "Morning Mary, where've ya bin, I've been waitin for ya to come in"

Mary is dumbstruck, "Errrr, alright Ed, just been down the shops, how are ya today?"

Eddie goes on to ask whether she fancies a cuppa, "I'll get one of the nurses to get ya one if ya want"

"Yes love, I'll have one, but just before we do, can I have a hug, it'd mean the world to me right now"

Mary wraps her arms around Eddie and squeezes with all her might. "Bloody hell woman ya gonna break me ribs"

"Please don't let go Ed, hold me for ever, I promise I won't ever let you go love"

Over Eddies shoulder Mary can see Nurse Thompson in the doorway with tears in her eyes, Mary mouths to her "it's a miracle, he's back."

They hold on to each other for what seems like ages and then Mary finally steps back from the bed. "That was beautiful Ed, maybe we can do that every day."

Eddie seems to go into a blank stare and asks what she wants and why she's in his room.

Mary drops back to earth with a bang, "you just called me Mary, you asked me where I've been, you can't have forgotten already"

She sits in the chair and starts to weep, what does she have to do to get him back, how long before he holds her again.

The nurse comes in and tries to console Mary, but it's an impossible task she is in bits and cannot be consoled.

Mary leaves the nursing home in despair, she's not sure she can take this any longer. She arrives back at the house and can't even recall getting on the bus or waiting at the stop.

In the early hours Mary is awoken by the ringing of the phone, she looks at it for a few seconds, scared to pick it up, there's only one reason her phone would be ringing in the early hours and she doesn't want to hear it.

She picks up the handset with shaking hands and slowly lifts it to her ear, "Hello."

"Hello Mrs Jones, it's Joanne, one of the nurses at the home, I'm afraid I've got some bad news for"

That was the last that Mary heard of the call, she collapsed into her bed and broke down sobbing, her whole body shaking uncontrollably. She grabbed tight hold of her pillow and dug her nails in as if trying to pull it apart with her tiny frail hands.

The rest of the night was a blur as memory after memory of Eddie bounced around her mind. The house suddenly seemed like an empty box, no life, no love, nothing but an empty box.

It was over a week before Eddie could be buried. They were going to hold the service at the same Church of All Saints where they were married.

The day came and Mary was taken to the church alone in a car following the hearse. In the hearse was just one bouquet, that simply said 'Ed' in red and white flowers. There was a small turn out of a few neighbours and a couple of people Eddie had worked with on the docks. There wasn't a family left to attend, no brothers, sisters or children, just Mary.

Mary thanked the people who had turned out at the church for Ed, but then went directly home after the cremation and made herself a cup of tea while she went through the old photographs again and again. As she flicked through them, she chatted to Eddie, "You were a proper hunk back then love, I miss you so much, you were, and always will be, my Eddie." She held a couple of photographs tight to her chest and sobbed.

Later that night Mary made her way to bed, saying goodnight to Eddie, she laid down with a heavy heart and turned out the bedside lamp.

Mary fell into a deep sleep and started to dream, in her dream she was walking along a harbour in the warm sunshine until she reached a gentleman in a stunning white uniform who guided her up the gang plank of a beautiful, brilliant white cruise ship and at the top stood Eddie, he held out his arms and Mary fell into them. He gave her a big smile, took her by the hand and asked her to sit down, he had somebody who was keen to see her. They talked for a minute or two before a couple of figures came through an open door and walked towards them. "Margi, Terry, Ohh my giddy Aunt! I must be in heaven; this is just perfect."

As she said those words, she heard a door close behind her and the ship gave a blast on its horn as if to signal the start of a new journey.

Printed in Great Britain
by Amazon